SOUL MATES

SOUL MATES

L. A. WEATHERLY

Barrington Stoke

First published in 2014 in Great Britain by
Barrington Stoke Ltd
18 Walker Street, Edinburgh, EH3 7LP

www.barringtonstoke.co.uk

ISBN: 978-1-78112-310-2

Printed in China by Leo

To my husband, who makes me
believe in soul mates

How can you miss someone you've never met?

I always know him by his eyes.

Sometimes we're on the deck of a ship together, in old-fashioned clothes. Or we stand in the shadow of the Pyramids. Or we watch a tropical sunset. It doesn't matter. I may not know his name, but his eyes are always the same – a deep, gentle brown. And the look in them as he turns to me is ... something I've never seen before.

Not in real life, anyway.

Tonight I dreamed about him again.

This time we're hiking in the snow. We both have on heavy coats, and he has his arm around me, to shield me from the cold.

"Don't worry," he says. He has to raise his voice over the wind. "We'll be all right."

It's so cold, and I know we're lost. But I'm not scared. Because we're together, and that means we can do anything.

"I'm not worried," I say. I stop and rest my hands on either side of his face. I kiss him. His lips are warm, even in the cold.

He grins through the snowflakes. "You could be a *little* worried," he says. "We're not home yet."

He's so beautiful. Maybe that's a funny word to use for a boy who's almost a man, but it's true. And as I look into his dark eyes I have a thousand memories.

It has always been him.

I start to touch his mouth with my finger. Then I gasp as an icy shiver runs down my spine. I glance around us, terrified of what I might see. But there are only snow-covered trees.

He takes my hand and we start to walk again, faster than before. "We'll be all right," he repeats.

His jaw looks hard now, and I know that he feels it, too. There's something out there. Something evil – jealous.

Something that will stop at nothing to tear us apart.

⊗∾⊗

"Carlton, New Mexico!"

I wake up with a gasp. My pulse is pounding. I'm on a Greyhound bus, with my face pressed up against a window. A fat lady snores in the seat next to me.

It was only a dream. For a second I want to cry. OK, part of it was scary, but I'd still give anything to be back in it again. The boy's face has already begun to fade from my mind – just like always. All I have left are his voice and eyes.

I swallow hard. His love for me was so clear in both.

Love. Something in me hardens, and I glare out the window at the dusty town. Yeah, right. As if love like that could ever be real anyway. Why do I keep dreaming about this stupid boy? He's been haunting me for years.

Along with that sense of something evil. I go cold as I remember. Then I shake my head, irritated. 'Get a grip, Iris,' I think.

As the bus pulls into the station I grab my backpack and climb over the sleeping fat lady. This is where I get off. It's as far as I could afford. I still have a long way to go, but I'm a few hundred miles closer now.

I'm the only one who gets off. The driver looks at me as I step out into the warm night air. "Got someone meeting you?" he asks.

"Sure, my aunt." The lie comes with ease. I've had a lot of chance to practise, these last few days. The bus driver nods – he's bored already. The doors slide shut and the bus pulls away into the night.

I go over to the vending machines. I don't have much money – only what I've managed to save. I check the change slot and find a quarter. Thank God. I add a few more coins and buy a Snickers bar.

As I eat, I stare at the highway. The cars are bright streaks of light heading west. Same as me.

I know where I'm going, and that almost makes me feel as if I belong somewhere. I haven't felt that way since Gran died and I got put into care. But I've been sure of where I need to go for a long time. I've never been there, but it feels like ... well, like there's a magnet, and it's pulling me there.

OK, I guess that's pretty crazy. But at least it's somewhere to go – as good a place as any. Because I am *not* going back into care. Ever. I think about that sleaze at the group home and shudder.

Not that anyone's going to come looking for me. Another 16-year-old runaway – who cares?

I swing my backpack over one shoulder and head towards the highway. It's summer and the wind is warm, even at night. It stirs at my long, dark hair. My feet kick up small clouds of dust with every step.

When I reach the side of the highway, I stop and stick out my thumb.

⊗⊗⊗

"We're just coming into Los Angeles," a woman's cheery voice says.

I open my eyes, still heavy with sleep. When I realise what I was dreaming, I wince. 'God, not *him* again,' I think. 'What exactly is wrong with me?'

The woman at the wheel of the car is middle-aged and chubby. "Sorry to wake you up," she says. "I thought you'd want to see the skyline." She takes a slurp of coffee.

"That's OK," I say. I've been lucky. I know it's stupid to hitchhike, but most people who picked me up were worried about me. One old lady scolded me all the way across Arizona, telling me how dangerous it is to hitch rides.

I sit up and stare at the long, smoggy skyline in wonder. I've actually done it. I've made it to Los Angeles – two thousand miles from Texas.

"Where in the city are you heading?" the woman asks. Then she grins. "Let me guess. You want to be an actress."

"No, I'm visiting my grandparents," I say. "They've got a place near Hollywood and Vine."

It's the only Los Angeles address I know. It's the same one everyone knows. But as I say it I stare up at the hills north of the city. And my pulse skips a beat as it hits me – that's where I'm going.

After the woman drops me off, I get a city bus. Then I walk for a long time. By late afternoon I'm on a road high above Los Angeles. I can see the entire city, and the big HOLLYWOOD sign a few hills over.

I'm not sure what to do. For so long, I've felt like I *have* to come to L. A. But why? I don't feel drawn to anything at all now. I have no idea why I'm up in these hills.

I walk on down the road. The sun is hot, my backpack heavy.

'I need to figure out what I'm going to do,' I think as I trudge along. 'I'll have to try and get a job somewhere.'

Coming up here was such a waste of time. I should be heading the other way, back down into the city. But for some reason I keep going, even though I'm getting more annoyed at myself with every step.

I'm just about to turn back when I come to an old iron gate. I stop and stare. It's tall, with spikes on top, and it's hanging off its hinges. On the other side of the gate is a long dirt track. There are weeds everywhere. And orange trees – I can smell them.

I hold onto the gate as I look in. There's a house at the end of the track. Big, like something a Hollywood star would have. It looks old and abandoned. I glance behind me. There's no one around.

'This is such a bad idea,' I tell myself. 'The place is probably full of druggies.'

But for some reason I really want to see the house up close. I hesitate – and then squeeze through a gap in the gate.

The only sounds are my footsteps and the wind in the trees. When I reach the house it's even older than I thought. Worn steps lead to the front door, and half the windows are boarded up.

I wipe the palms of my hands on my jeans. All of a sudden I feel excited – nervous. But why? It's only an old house.

I want to go inside so much that it scares me a little. There's an old-fashioned well nearby, and I go over, rest my hands on the cool stone and look down. From far away, my face stares back at me.

There's a bucket on a chain. When I try it, the pulley still works, but the wooden bucket has rotted away. Big surprise.

Come in.

I jump and stare at the house, my eyes wide. It's like it *spoke* to me. No, this is way too freaky! I snatch up my backpack and start to leave – but then I pause and look back. My pulse skips another beat.

I have to see what's inside.

I can't stop myself. I head towards the house and walk up the creaky steps.

The front door opens when I try it. Somehow I'm not surprised. My heart pounds as I walk inside. The house is cool and dusty. Everything's in shadow. I can see the shapes of furniture covered in sheets, like ghosts.

It doesn't feel like I'm alone.

"Hello?" I call out, and then I wish I hadn't. My voice sounds shaky. Scared.

I edge forward. The floor creaks. There's a small pattering sound and I stop short. Then I relax. 'Just a mouse, Iris,' I think. 'Don't be a baby.'

At last my eyes grow used to the dim light and I can see the house in more detail. It looks as if no one has been here in years. But that *can't* be true. Someone would have found this place and used it.

All of a sudden, my neck prickles. I spin round. There's only the long shape of a sofa covered with a sheet. I gulp as I look at it, thinking someone might sit up, dragging the sheet with them.

Nothing.

The house is so silent. Why am I doing this? If I were smart, I'd leave. Yet it feels as if something is waiting for me – something so close, but just out of my reach. I almost want to cry with frustration.

"OK, if there's a reason I'm here, just *tell* me, or I'm gone," I say out loud. I don't know who I'm talking to.

But something responds.

When I came in, I left the front door open – sunlight has been shining in. Now the light starts to fade. As I realise why ... I go cold.

The front door is closing.

My mouth feels gritty with fear as the room darkens. The latch gives a faint *click* as it closes. The sound wakes me up. I sprint for the door, but the knob won't turn.

I pound my fist on the wood. "No! Let me out!"

Unseen hands struggle with me. I can *almost* hear something, like a voice just out of earshot. Oh God, I'm going crazy. "Stop!" I shout. "I have to get *out* of here!"

Something solid that I can't see blocks my path. This can't be happening! I turn and race the other way. A kitchen. There's a back door – I throw myself at it with a gasp of relief.

But whatever's in the house is faster. Running footsteps gain on me. As I grab the kitchen doorknob I feel a sharp jolt up my arm. I scream and jerk my hand away.

And that's when I see the boy.

He's standing by the door and he looks as stunned as I am. For a second I can't speak. He wasn't there before. He *wasn't*.

The boy is about 17, with sandy hair and brown eyes. He doesn't move as we stare at each other. "I, um – didn't mean to scare you," he says at last. "I'm very sorry –" He starts to reach towards me. I yank away.

"Don't touch me," I snap, to hide my fear. "Who the hell are you?"

The boy's hair is combed back from his face. It shows off his high cheekbones. He's wearing tan trousers, and a white shirt with a sharp collar. His sleeves are rolled up. On one wrist is a watch with a leather strap.

He swallows and puts his hands in his pockets. He's still watching me – as if he'll never be able to look away. "I'm Nate," he says. "I'm sorry – I was just afraid you'd leave. You didn't seem to see me at first ..."

My throat is dry. This cannot be real. "What exactly are you?" I demand.

He blinks. "What *am* I?"

"A ghost? What?"

He looks confused. "No. I thought maybe *you* were a ghost."

"Yeah?" I say. "Well, you didn't seem too scared, for someone who thought he'd seen a ghost. That *was* you, fighting with me at the front door, right?" My voice sounds hard, like I'm not scared at all. But I've noticed how much stronger than me Nate looks. How firm across the shoulders.

He could do anything he wanted, and I couldn't stop him.

Nate's still gazing at me. "Yes, that was me," he admits. "And no, I wasn't scared. Not of *you*. How could I be?"

His eyes are very brown, with long lashes. For a second I'm sure I've seen them before.

Then I shake myself. This is *not* the time to be distracted by a boy's eyes!

I grip the strap of my backpack. "Well, you *better* be scared of me," I growl. "Because I promise you, if you lay one hand on me –"

Nate looks alarmed. He takes a step back with his hands up. "Whoa, whoa. I'm not going to – my God, is *that* what you think?"

All of a sudden I'm furious. "What the hell am I supposed to think?" I yell. "Jesus, I'm stuck here in this creepy house, with *you* trying to keep me inside! That's it, I'm out of here."

Before he can answer, I turn and stride back towards the front door. "Wait!" he calls. I hear him coming after me.

"Do *not* try to stop me," I say. "I mean it. I've got a knife."

Nate darts around in front of me. "*Wait.* Please." He touches my arm.

I stop and glare at him. Why don't I want to jerk away?

Nate hesitates and then lets his hand drop. "Look, I won't stop you if you really want to leave, but ... but don't you ...?" He trails off. He's staring at me so hard that I feel nervous.

"Don't I what?" I say.

At first I think he's not going to answer. "Don't you know me?" he asks at last. His voice is shy. It sounds weird, coming from such a big, confident-looking guy.

I almost say yes, but then I bite the word back. How can I know him? I've never even seen him before! Yet I want to reach for his hand and take it in mine.

This scares me almost more than anything else that's happened. I'm seriously going insane. "No, I do not know you." My voice is harsh. "Now will you get out of my way?"

His shoulders sag. "Fine," he says. "I'm sorry. I just thought ... Forget it. I was wrong, I guess."

I head for the door. It feels like I have to rush before I change my mind.

"Wait!" he calls again. I stop, but don't look back. "Could you just tell me your name?" he asks.

I don't know why I answer. "Iris," I say, after a pause.

When I turn around Nate's still standing there. His hands are at his sides, balled into fists. He nods, gazing at me as if he's memorising every detail.

"That's a pretty name," he says. His voice is soft.

I swallow hard. I start to reach for the door, then snap my hand away. "Will it do that *thing* again?"

Nate glances at his hand. Maybe the jolt from the kitchen door hurt him, too. "I don't think so," he says. "We both touched the doorknob at the same time. It was as if ... as if my hand went *through* yours for a second."

I stare at him. Whatever he is, he's not a ghost – he's as solid as I am. "But that's impossible," I say weakly.

His eyes meet mine. "Yeah," he says. He sounds almost bitter. "I suppose maybe a lot of things are."

I feel shaken. Why does it hurt me so much to see that look on his face? Why do I want to go back and comfort him? This is all way too weird.

I throw open the door and leave.

⟨3⟩

As I hurry along the dirt track I break into a run. Everything has gone oddly still. For a confused second I think the gate looks whole and unbroken. Then it's the same as I remember again.

I shove myself out through the gap. I keep thinking I'll hear Nate's voice – feel his hand on my arm.

Nothing happens.

Am I sad? Or relieved? I don't stop to wonder – I just head down the main road as fast as I can. At first I keep looking back over my shoulder. Each time I do, the road is empty.

At last the gate is out of sight. The world seems back to normal. When I come to a large rock at the side of the road, I let out a shaky breath and sit down. God, what *happened* back there?

I pull my water from my pack and take a long sip. My hand's trembling. As I put the bottle back, I remember how I told Nate I had a knife. I was lying. But I think maybe he'd have left me alone anyway. He seemed ... nice.

I shake my head, furious with myself. Yeah, right – *nice*. Just like that creep at the group home.

Besides, there's no way any of this had been real. Probably just a dream.

A dream.

All of a sudden, I freeze. My head starts to pound as memories come rushing back. The boy in my dream, walking through the snow with me. The feel of his lips on mine. The look in his eyes as he teases me.

His face always fades when I wake up, but not his eyes. They're so gentle. So dark and warm. "Oh my God," I whisper as it hits me.

I just met the boy I've been in love with for years.

I'm positive I've gone insane. But nothing on the planet could stop me from going back to the house now. I jog down the road. When I reach the gate I stop in my tracks and stare.

It still looks old, but it's not falling down any more – its metal bars are whole again. There's a padlock on them. I gape in confusion – I squeezed through just minutes ago. *What* is going on?

Then a terrible thought comes. What if Nate isn't in the house any more? What if I've missed him – forever?

My pulse races in panic. I climb over the gate and drop to the ground. I sprint down the dirt track. The house still seems abandoned, but it looks newer, too. The steps don't creak as I run up them.

"Nate!" I yell as I go in. "*Nate!*"

He's there. He's slumped on the sofa with his head low and his hands covering his face. I'm so relieved that I can't speak.

All of a sudden I feel shy. I perch on the sofa beside him and wait for him to look up. I can't stop staring at his profile – his straight nose, the slight curve of his lips. Oh my God, he's *real*. He's here.

Nate doesn't move. After a minute I clear my throat. "Nate? Um ... Listen, I was wrong, OK? When I said I didn't know you."

He sighs and doesn't look up. I hesitate, then put my hand on his arm. His skin is warm and firm, just like in hundreds of my dreams. I feel dizzy. I can't believe this is happening.

"I'm so sorry," I tell him. "Of course I know you. I'd know you anywhere. This all just seems so impossible that I –"

Suddenly he stands up. "You *idiot!*" he snaps. I blink with hurt ... but he's talking to himself. "To find her at last and then *lose* her again," he goes on. "No, this can't happen. I've got to go after her!"

"Wait, I'm right here!" I jump up and grab his arm.

He takes off for the door as if I'm not even there. In another second he's outside and down the steps. "Iris!" he calls. "*Iris!*"

I run after him. When he reaches the gate it's still locked. He starts to climb, and fear grips me. If he leaves this place it feels as if he might vanish for good.

I dart in front of him. "Stop! No!" I try to push him away, struggling as hard as I can.

Nate pauses, his dark eyes wide as he looks around. "Wait. I thought I felt ..."

"Me!" I yell. "You felt me!" In the distance I can see a few old cars on the main road. They're tall and funny-looking, with narrow tyres.

Nate shakes his head and starts to climb again. "No!" I shout. Then I remember how he first appeared. We both touched the doorknob at the same time. 'It was as if my hand went through yours ...'

I don't stop to think. I put my hand on the gate. Not on Nate's hand – I'm focussing on the metal bars – but his hand's in the way.

My hand gives a shiver and passes right through Nate's.

⚜ 4 ⚜

The cars on the road vanish. I shriek as some unseen force knocks me away from the gate. I land on my back in the grass hard.

Oh God, that *hurt*. I feel like a million volts of power just went through me. I wince as I lift myself up on my elbows.

Nate's been knocked back, too. He's lying sprawled on the grass. "Iris!" he cries. He clambers up, rushes over and kneels beside me. His sandy hair looks wild and ruffled.

"Are you all right? But – but how did you –?" He breaks off and stares at me.

I sit up. "I'm fine," I say. My voice is shaky.

Everything's gone so still, as if the sun's frozen in the sky. Even the birds aren't singing any more. I glance at the road, wondering where the cars went.

Why am I thinking about *cars*, when Nate's right here?

I feel shy again. I clear my throat. "You, um – couldn't see me until I put my hand on yours," I tell him.

"Just like you couldn't see *me* before," he whispers. His hand is near mine on the grass. He looks down at them. So do I. His looks large – strong. He hesitates ... and then puts his hand over mine.

This time we both stay solid. At the feel of his warm fingers, I swallow hard.

Nate keeps looking down at our hands. His cheeks turn red. "Iris, I have no idea what's going on. All I know is that you're going to think I'm crazy. I've been dreaming about you. For years now."

I gasp. "You *have*? I've been dreaming about you too!"

His head snaps up. "Really? But you said you didn't know me!"

"No, I was wrong, I – I definitely know you." My mouth feels dry. "I dream about you all the time. Sometimes we're walking through the snow, or maybe standing on a tropical beach, or walking through a city –"

He grips my fingers hard. "Or sailing on a ship, or looking at the Pyramids, or a thousand other things," he finishes. "Yes! It's the same for me."

Neither of us says what else is in the dreams – the love we have for each other. Does Nate have *that* in his dreams, too? My face grows hot. There is no way I'm going to ask.

It's so quiet. Nate starts to say something else. Then he swallows and looks down, at our two hands.

I can't help staring at him. This really isn't a dream. Nate isn't a stranger to me. I *know* him, inside and out. How stubborn he can be. His sense of humour. How gentle his hands are when he strokes them across my skin – how his touch makes me feel like I'm catching fire.

'Nate, I've missed you so much,' I think. That's what it feels like – as if I've been missing him my whole life. All I want to do is wrap my arms around him.

But what if I've got this wrong? He'll think I'm insane, even if he *has* been dreaming about me. The thought brings me back to reality with a thud. I try to laugh.

"So, um ... this is kind of strange," I say.

Nate seems to realise he's still holding my hand. He lets go and sits up. "And how!" He shakes his head and gazes at me. "I can't believe you're actually *real*. This is just ... Where do you live?"

I hate talking about anything personal. It hurts too much. But with Nate, for some reason I don't mind. "Texas, for the most part," I say. "Or I did. I ran away. I, um ... I've been in care since I was seven."

He frowns. "In care?"

"You know. Like, foster parents. At first I lived with my grandmother, but she died. Then my mother gave me up, but I was too old for anyone to want to adopt me by then, so ..."

Nate looks shocked. "Your mother gave you up?" he repeats.

"Yeah. She – has problems. No big loss." I force a laugh. "What about you?" I ask.

"No, wait," Nate says. His brown eyes are full of concern. "Why did you run away?"

I think of the creep at the group home and wince. I don't want Nate to know that someone was so ... slimy with me. "I just got tired of it," I say. I manage a smile and try to change the subject. "Come on, tell me about you."

I know Nate gets that there's something I don't want to talk about. For a second I think he's going to take my hand again, but he doesn't.

"Me? Very boring subject," he says instead.

'I don't believe you,' I think. 'Nothing about you could possibly be boring.'

Nate picks a blade of grass and plays with it. "I live a few miles from here," he says. "I've got parents ... a little sister named Ruth. I'll be a senior next year. I'm supposed to be thinking about college, but ..." He shrugs a shoulder.

"You don't want to go?"

He makes a face and throws the grass away. "My dad and I argue about it a lot. And to be honest, I know he's right. It makes me feel like a real sap."

'A real *what?*' I almost ask, but Nate's still talking. "I can't help it," he says. "I've never been that interested in college. To tell you the truth –" He glances at me and breaks off.

"What?" I ask. My pulse has started to race at the look in his eyes.

Nate's voice is low. "To tell you the truth, Iris ... I've never been interested in anything much, except trying to find you. I dream about you all the time – even when I'm not asleep."

My mouth feels like cotton. "I know," I whisper. "Me too, about you."

He laughs shakily and pushes his hair back. "I've never told anyone about you, but my family thinks I'm screwy anyway," he says. "I spend hours looking at maps – wondering where you might be. When I leave high school – well, I had planned just to hit the road and look for you. I knew you might not even be real, but I still had to try and find you."

"And now you have." I almost can't say the words. He has to feel the same way about me as I do about him – he *has* to.

But does he?

Nate sounds hoarse. "Yeah. By some incredible miracle ... I have."

We're sitting close enough to touch. The hairs on his arm look golden in the sunlight. Nate gazes at my lips. For a second he hesitates ... and then he starts to lean towards me. My heart goes wild in my chest.

He seems to catch himself. He looks shaken as he jumps to his feet.

"Come on," he says. He tries to smile. "What do you say we explore this place a little?"

⚭5⚭

Nate and I stand side by side as we peer into the well. From far away, our two faces gaze back. His hair is so sandy, and mine's so dark.

We look as if we belong together.

'Stop that right now,' I order myself. Nate could have kissed me and didn't. That kind of says it all, doesn't it? Maybe he just sees me as a friend.

Or maybe meeting me in real life isn't as good as in his dreams.

"That's funny," Nate says, out of the blue.

I shove away my last thought as hard as I can. "What's funny?"

Nate's frown is one I've seen a thousand times. "The bucket," he says. "Look."

He works the pulley, and my eyes widen. The bucket's brand new. "But it wasn't even *there* before!" I burst out. "It was all rotted away."

"Before? When do you mean?"

I look back at the gate. Is my mind playing tricks, or is it even newer now?

"When I came here the first time," I say, "the house looked older, and the gate was falling down. The bucket was totally rotted away."

Nate's frown deepens as he studies the bucket. "And when *I* came here, the bucket was old, but still in one piece."

It would take years for a bucket to rot away, wouldn't it? Just like it would take years for an iron gate to fall down. I lick my lips. "How – how long were you in the house before I first got here?"

He glances at his watch. "Hands have stopped," he mutters. "I don't know – ten minutes? I've passed this old place a hundred times, but today it felt like I *had* to go inside."

35

We stare at each other. This is all so weird. We've not even discussed the way we couldn't see each other at first. Yet neither of us says anything. I guess it feels too strange to talk about.

After a long pause, Nate puts the bucket back into place. "I was going to get us some water, but ..." He shrugs, looking uneasy.

I know what he means. That well is giving me the creeps. I don't know why. The house and the yard seem fine, even with everything so still and quiet. But the well is like a dark, hungry mouth, ready to eat us up. I shiver and take a step back.

Nate touches my arm. "Why don't we go inside? It's cooler in there anyway."

I feel myself relax at his touch. Somehow, just having him standing there next to me is a comfort.

I clear my throat and nod. "Yeah. Good idea."

∾∾∾

Nate and I walk around the house, checking out every room. Everything looks newer now, though the furniture is still covered with sheets.

"I wonder who owned this place?" I say. We're standing in a bathroom downstairs. There's an old-fashioned bathtub with high sides.

"I don't know," Nate says. "It's been abandoned for as long as I've loved here." The second the words are out, his cheeks redden. "I mean ... *lived* here," he says after a pause.

I stare at him, then look back at the tub. That had to be just a slip of the tongue, right?

Nate crosses his arms over his chest. "How about we look upstairs?" he suggests weakly.

We end up in what I guess was a bedroom, though it's empty now. There's a window seat with a view of the overgrown front yard. We sit down. The orange trees are in bloom. We can't see the well, and I'm glad.

"Would you tell me more about you?" Nate looks at me with a crooked smile. "Please," he adds. "I want to know everything."

"OK," I reply. "But you have to tell me everything, too."

I talk to him more than I ever have to anyone. I tell him about the foster homes I've been in. What it was like with Gran. I even manage to talk about the creep back in Texas.

He was one of the adults at the group home. And he was always finding ways to touch me. Like, he'd rub up against me from behind. Touch my arm longer than he should. Stroke the small of my back – or even lower.

Nate's brown eyes are full of concern. He also looks completely furious. "So what happened?" he asks in a low voice.

I have a bad taste in my mouth. "Last week we were alone. I tried to go upstairs, and he said I had to pay a toll first. He had his arm round me, holding me against him. He pretended he was just playing around, but he wasn't."

I fall silent as I remember. I could tell he wasn't joking. I could tell how ... excited he was. It was horrible.

I can see Nate's guessed this. One of his hands is a fist. "What did you do?"

"One of the other adults came home then. But before that, I kneed him as hard as I could."

Nate gives a short, surprised laugh. "Good."

"Everyone really respected him, though," I say. "I knew no one would believe me, and he'd keep trying. So I ran away. Besides, I ..." I shrug and my cheeks turn hot. "Well, I've always felt like I have to come here."

"I'm very glad you did," Nate murmurs. His fist is still tight. I have a feeling the creep won't enjoy it much if Nate ever meets him. Then Nate clears his throat. "And Iris ... I think you're one of the bravest people I know."

My cheeks redden further, with joy this time.

Nate tells me about his life, too. His family – going to school. How he loves the outdoors. "Hiking up in the mountains is so …" He stops as he searches for the right word. "… peaceful," he finishes. "Just me and the trees and the sky."

I love the look on his face as he's talking about this. And I know it already – just like I know his grin, and how his eyes look when he's serious.

I know all of him.

We talk for a long time, though the shadows outside never move. We share so much – it feels as if I could keep talking to this boy for ever, and never run out of things to say.

"You know, um … those dreams we've both had?" I ask at last. It's something we haven't discussed.

Nate goes still. "Yeah?"

It's hard to say, but I want him to know. "So often, they've felt like the only good thing in my life. The only thing that makes me happy."

"I'm glad." Nate's voice is husky. "I mean, not that they're the only good thing. But that they make you happy. I feel the same. If it wasn't for the dreams –" He stops.

"Really?" I'm surprised. "But your life sounds so nice!"

"I know – I'm lucky. You've had such a hard time, Iris. I wish I could erase all the bad things. But even so, I – Oh, hell." Nate shoves a hand through his hair. "Sorry," he adds.

I smile a little. Sorry, for saying 'hell'?

Nate goes on. "The thing is … I've always felt so out of place. As if I'm not really supposed to be here, or as if … This probably sounds like a lot of hooey."

I don't know what 'hooey' means, but I still understand. "No, it doesn't!" I tell him. My chest is tight. "Nate, I feel exactly the same way. The dreams are the only time when –"

"When everything feels right," he finishes.

I nod, unable to speak.

"But ... no, that's not quite true, is it?" he adds in a low voice. "Because there's this right now, too. With you."

Our gazes meet. Nate looks very serious, with no smile in sight. My heart's beating hard ... because neither of us can seem to turn away. As I see the look in his dark eyes, time stops. Everything stops. I think I've forgotten how to breathe.

I'll die if I touch him. I'll die if I don't.

I reach out and rest my hand on his arm. I rub it gently, feeling the warmth of his skin – the firm muscle underneath.

"Nate," I whisper.

At first he doesn't move, and I want to disappear. I've somehow gotten it wrong.

Then I see him swallow. "Slap me if I'm out of line, because I can't stop myself any more," he mutters – and he strokes his hands through my hair and kisses me.

I've never wanted anyone to kiss me before. But Nate's mouth feels like it was made to fit against mine. I close my eyes, melting in the warmth of his lips.

The kiss stays tender. At last Nate pulls away a little. "Was it – was it all right that I did that?" he asks. "You can still slap me if you want."

My hand is resting against his chest. I can feel his heart pounding. 'I've found him again,' I think in wonder. 'And I am never letting him go.'

I clear my throat. "No slap," I tell him. "And yes, it was very all right. In fact ... I don't think you should stop."

I bring his head back down to mine and we kiss again. And again. Our lips feel hot against each other now. I'm drowning – I can never get enough of him. Nate's arms are tight around me. He kisses my lips, my hair. "I've got to tell you something – please don't think I'm crazy," he gasps.

He pulls away to look at me. The look on his face is almost fierce. "I love you, Iris. I always have, from the very first dream. There's no one else for me but you – not ever."

"I love you, too." I'm nearly crying. I don't even know why. "Nate, it's always been you. Even when I didn't know your name ... I knew we belonged to each other."

He lets out a long, shuddering breath. He puts both arms around me and holds me close. I press tight against him. I can't tell which heartbeat is his and which is mine.

After a long time he kisses my head.

"Tell me again," he whispers.

❦ 6 ❦

Nate's leaning against the wall with his arms around me. I have my head on his chest. I listen to the beat of his heart through his soft white shirt, and I stroke my hand up and down his arm.

I didn't know that such happiness even existed.

"I still can't believe this is real," Nate says. "When I first saw you, I thought it was just another dream."

"I know." I sit up and gaze at him. I know every line and curve of his face. How could it have ever faded from my mind? I lean over and kiss him. His lips feel so right.

He grins and kisses me back. "You know, I could get used to this," he whispers against my mouth.

"Me too," I say. But all at once a chill touches me. Because there's something in the dreams we've forgotten, isn't there?

That sense of something watching us … Something evil.

I shiver, and Nate frowns in concern. "Iris? What is it?"

I shake my head, not wanting to break the mood. "Nothing," I say at last. "It's just that I want this to last for ever, and …" I can't finish.

"It will," Nate says. He squeezes my hand. "Now that we've found each other, do you think I'm ever letting you go?"

I hope he's right. I gaze out at the orange trees. The sun still hasn't moved. Not in all the time we've been up here.

"I wonder what happened to the cars?" I say.

Nate has his arms around me again – he's kissing my cheek, my hair … "What cars?" he murmurs.

46

It feels as if everything could disappear if we're not careful. But something makes me say it. "The funny old-timey ones. They were driving down the road when you saw me appear out by the gate. Then they just – vanished."

Nate sits up a little, looking confused. "Old-timey?" he repeats. "What do you mean?"

I shrug. "You know. They were black – kind of tall. Thin tyres. The roofs were made of canvas, I think." When I see the way he's looking at me, I lick my lips. "What?"

"Iris ... those just sound like ordinary flivvers."

"Ordinary *what*?"

"Flivvers. Model Ts." He frowns. "You must have heard of the Model T Ford. They're everywhere."

"No, they're not," I say in confusion. "The only people who still drive cars like that do it for a hobby. I saw a bunch of them at an antique fair once ..." I trail off as we stare at each other. I have a very bad feeling.

Nate grips my hand. His voice is intense. "Tell me what year it is."

When I tell him, his face turns white. "Oh, my God," he says.

"What? What year do *you* think it is?"

"Iris, it's 1922! Harding is president. The Great War finished four years ago."

The Great War? I stare at Nate's watch, at his tan trousers and white shirt. It's a button-down shirt with a sharp collar. He looks great. But ... now that I think about it, it's all kind of formal for a teenage boy, isn't it? And there's the way his hair's combed back – the strange words he's used a few times.

"You're – you're really from the past." I can barely say it.

Nate's staring at my jeans and T-shirt. He looks dazed. "I thought you were dressed as a boy because you'd run away," he says.

I blink. "Dressed as a boy?"

"You look beautiful," he jumps in. "No, you look ... stunning. Iris, I don't care what you wear! I just – I didn't imagine that it was because you're from the future. It's not really the first thing that comes to mind."

The future. I feel dizzy as I think about everything else that's changed between his time and mine. Computers. The Internet. TV. How come we didn't talk about any of that stuff? But of course we didn't. We just talked about us.

My hands are cold. "We're from different worlds."

"Different times," Nate says.

"It's the same thing!" I stand up, too upset to stay still. "Oh my God, I don't believe this. I'm in love with a boy from almost a hundred years ago!

A boy who –" I stop short as I look at him. I feel faint.

I'm in love with a boy who cannot still be alive in my own time. And if he was, he'd be a little old man.

"No," I whisper.

Nate's on his feet in seconds. He grips my arms. "Stop," he says. "We will figure this out, I promise you. We *will* be together, Iris."

I hardly hear him. All I can think is how unfair this is. How can we be together? Sooner or later, we'll have to return to our own times. I'm about to be hurt again, worse than ever in my whole life. Why didn't I guess that, the second I found Nate, fate would snatch him away again?

No. Forget it. I'm not going through this.

"You figure it out," I tell him. My voice has gone hard, like when we first met. "I'm getting out of here."

❦ 7 ❧

Nate's jaw drops. "*What?*"

I've already pulled away from him and started for the door. He lunges after me and grips my arm. "Iris, *stop*! You can't just –"

I jerk away. "Can't just what? Refuse to go through this kind of pain? Watch me!"

His face has gone stiff with hurt. "You'd really just walk away from this? Away from us?"

My heart is breaking. I ignore it. "What 'us'?" I snap. "For there to be an 'us', we kind of have to be in the same time!"

"We're here now!" he shouts.

"And where is *here*?" I look around wildly. "This is some sort of – of weird in-between time! The sun hasn't moved in hours, do you realise that? Whatever this place is, it isn't real!"

Nate's dark eyes flash. "*I* am real," he says in a low voice. "And *you* are real. And *this* – this is real."

He takes me in his arms and kisses me. His lips are hot, demanding. I feel like I'm falling – floating into nothing. Before I know it, I'm holding on to his shoulders and kissing him back as hard as I can. His warm mouth moves down to my neck and I think I might faint.

"That ... isn't fair." It's an effort to get the words out.

"No, I don't play fair when my life is at stake." He kisses my lips again, so hard it almost hurts. I stroke my hands through his soft sandy hair, hardly aware I'm doing it. "Tell me you're still leaving," he mutters between kisses. "Tell me you'd really walk away from me."

I can't say the words. I should have known from my dreams that Nate wouldn't let me go without a fight. 'But it will hurt so much more if I stay,' I think.

And then I feel something that turns my blood to ice.

A dark, clammy coldness. It's not close yet, but I can feel it heading towards us. Something evil ... and jealous.

I can tell Nate feels it too. All of a sudden he straightens up, his eyes wide. His arms tighten around me as if he's trying to protect me. "The rest of the dream," he murmurs.

I should be scared. Instead my fists clench. And I know now that I'll do whatever it takes to save what Nate and I have. Maybe I was going to leave on my own, but I will *not* let something else tear us apart.

"OK, you were right – I can't leave you," I tell Nate in a rush. I sound angry at him. Maybe I am, for making me love him this much. "Whatever this thing is, we have to fight it," I say. "We have to be together, no matter what."

Nate lets out a breath. "Thank God – don't scare me like that again." He starts to touch my face and then stops. The chill in the room is stronger now. The unseen danger is speeding towards us like a bullet.

"Come on!" he says. He grips my hand as he runs for the door. We pound down the stairs and past the living room, then out into the unending sunshine.

"Nate, no!" I gasp, when I see he's heading for the gate.

"We have to! We have to find out what's going on, and fast." We skid to a halt. "All right, you saw the cars vanish – so I think you're right; we're in some kind of in-between time here," he tells me, in a rush. "But what happens if we go over the gate together at the exact same moment?"

I swallow. The last time I left, Nate couldn't see me when I came back. What if that happens again, and I stay a ghost to him? But the air outside feels icy too, now. Somehow I know that the thing is coming *here*, to this empty house.

Beyond the gate feels like the only place we might be safe.

"All right, let's do it," I say.

We climb the gate side by side. At the top we swing ourselves over, careful to avoid the spikes. The road stretches out before us. It's empty.

"Ready?" Nate reaches a hand out to me. I grip it as hard as I can as I balance myself.

"Ready," I say, and we drop off the gate, holding on tight to each other.

❧ 8 ❧

I land on the road with a thud and roll a little. One second Nate's hand is holding mine, the next it isn't.

He's gone.

"No!" I cry. I scramble up and stare around me. The world has come back to life. I can feel a breeze on my face, see clouds moving in the sky. A truck passes with a honk, and I jump back from the road. It's a modern 4x4.

I'm in my own time. I spin towards the house, terrified that somehow it'll be gone. But it's still there, older again, with a falling-down gate.

'Don't panic,' I tell myself. 'The same thing must have happened in Nate's time. He'll just go back inside when I'm not there.' The thought calms me down.

But when I squeeze my way through the gate, it's like I've entered a tornado. A cold wind screams and howls as it whips at my hair and clothes. The sun is gone. There's only an eerie silver moonlight.

I can't see Nate anywhere.

He has to be here – he *has* to be. "Nate!" I shout. The wind snatches my voice away. "*Nate!*"

No answer. The house – maybe he's in there! I start for it, but in this raging wind it's a battle. I gasp and keep going, pushing as hard as I can against the wind. "Nate! Please answer me!" I call.

The wind grows stronger, until I can't take another step. I grit my teeth and try anyway. Then I hear a high-pitched giggle. It seems to come from all directions.

My skin turns cold. This isn't just a storm. Whatever that thing in our dreams is, it's here. "Let me go!" I shout. "I have to find him!"

'Have to find him,' my voice bounces back. It sounds like it's mocking me. Then the giggle comes again, louder. I turn to see who's there. There's nothing but the trees. Their branches are completely still in the silver light, even in the wind.

And then I see the well.

The strange wind shrieks around me as I stare at it. I shudder as I remember how it felt like a mouth ready to eat us up. I can see every grey stone in the moonlight.

'Something very bad is going to happen,' I think.

I take a step back and hug myself tight. "Oh God, Nate, where are you?" I whisper.

"Wouldn't you like to know?" a soft voice mocks.

I yelp and spin round. There's no one there.

"I could tell you ... if I felt like it," the voice says. Something cool touches my arm. The giggle comes again as I jerk away.

"Keep away from me!" I snarl. "Where's Nate? What have you done with –?"

Thunder roars in my ears. I cry out as I'm thrown onto my back. For a second the world goes white with pain. It feels like I've stuck my finger into a plug – as if my hair must be standing on end.

"Iris!" a voice shouts. "Are you all right?" When I open my eyes, Nate is there on the grass beside me. His face is tense with fear.

I throw myself into his arms. He catches me and holds me tight.

"I thought I'd never see you again!" I gasp against his neck.

"I know. Me too," he says, as he strokes my hair. "I was a ghost to you again. Then my hand passed through yours ... The blast was –" He stops, looking shaken.

The wind has died down now. As we pull apart I look around, scared of what might be watching us. There's nothing there.

"What – what *was* that thing?" I ask as we get up. "Could you see it?"

Nate shakes his head. "No, but I could hear it, and feel the wind. I think maybe it's gone for now."

I think of that creepy giggle and shiver. "Not for long, I bet."

"I'm sure you're right."

Our eyes meet. I can tell we're both thinking that we don't have a clue what to do when it returns. Hiding won't do much good – whatever this thing is, it would find us in an instant. Weapons seem pretty useless, too. How do you fight wind, or a voice? 'Maybe it can't hurt us if it's only a ghost,' I think.

But deep down I have a terrible feeling that it's something a lot worse.

Nate swallows. "Iris, listen – when we jumped down from the gate, I returned to my own time. I saw a car, that's how I knew. In fact, it almost hit me."

I nod. "Me too," I say. "I mean I saw a car from my own time."

He takes my hands, then brings them to his lips and kisses them. The look in his dark eyes is tearing me apart. "Please hear me out," he says softly. "I think you should forget about me and go back to your own time."

"*What?*" I gape at him. "Nate, no way!"

"Listen to me!" he says. "In the dreams, it feels like this thing hates *us*. Not you, or me, just the two of us together. If you go back to your own time, I don't think it'll follow you."

I'm close to tears, but also furious. "So we should just give up?" I yell. "That's your plan? What about when you stopped me from leaving, upstairs? Did you not *mean* any of that?"

"Of course I meant it!" He grips my face in his hands. "Iris, my God – I've spent half my life longing for you, and I didn't even know if you were real! But when we were upstairs, I didn't know we were in danger – that *you* were in danger. If it means you can be safe –" He breaks off.

I start to argue, and stop as it hits me. If I go back to my own time, then Nate will return to his. *He'll* be safe, too. The thought of being without him makes me feel sick … but I can do it if it's the only way to save him.

Then I see the look in his eyes. "Wait," I gasp. "You're planning on staying here, aren't you? You're trying to send *me* away, but you're staying!"

Nate winces. He doesn't deny it. "I just thought … if I stay and fight this thing, then maybe we can still be together, somehow, somewhere," he says in a low voice. "I've got to at least try."

I'm not sure how it's possible to be this angry at someone I love so much. "Well, forget it," I snap. "I don't know what girls in the 1920s are like, but I am *not* going to just run away and leave you here. If you're staying, then I am too. End of story – deal with it."

Nate gives a tiny smile as he studies me. "'Deal with it'?" he repeats, after a pause.

"It's a saying from my time. It means –"

"I think I can gather what it means." He sighs and rests his head on mine. I put my arms around him. "I should have known from the dreams that you wouldn't go," he says. "You've always been stubborn."

"Me?" I rest my hand against his cheek. He turns his head and presses his lips against my palm, and my heart skips a beat. "*You're* the stubborn one," I whisper.

"I'm giving in to you now," he says.

"There's no 'giving in'," I tell him. "You couldn't make me leave if you tried."

His voice is soft. "No. And I don't want to try any more. You're right, Iris. Whatever happens, we'll face it together."

He kisses me deeply then, and despite everything, I find myself getting lost in it. The feel of our mouths moving together. The solid heat of his body against mine. 'Nate, you're worth everything – no matter what,' I think.

And then we both stiffen. An icy chill has settled over us.

"How sweet," a voice sneers.

We turn as one. I hold back a scream.

A pale hand is coming out of the well. As we watch, it grips the stones and pulls. A little girl's face appears. It's a terrible, clammy white. Her eyes are even worse – they're pure black with no pupils.

And they're full of hatred.

The creature swings herself over the side of the well and sits there with her legs dangling. She has long blonde hair, and she wears an old-fashioned dress with a sash.

"Stupid, but sweet," she says in a high voice. She smiles and I shudder – her teeth are pointed, like a cat's.

Nate moves so that he's in front of me. "Who are you?" he demands.

She smiles and hops to the ground. "You can call me Sybil. It's not my name, but close enough. But *what* am I is a better question." She giggles. "The answer is that I'm your worst dream come true. Because you two know all about dreams, don't you?"

Neither of us responds. I watch in sick fascination as the ... thing comes towards us. She's only about as tall as a four-year-old.

"To tell you the truth, it's been very annoying," Sybil says. I grip Nate's arm and feel how he tenses as we wait to see what she'll do. "You just could *not* live without each other, could you?" she goes on.

"What do you mean?" I snap.

Sybil's black eyes burn into mine. "You really haven't figured it out yet?"

"If you've got something to say, spill it," Nate snaps.

"Oh, I will," she tells him. "But first ... I think we're just a little too cosy."

The wind returns. It howls past, pulling me away from Nate.

"No!" I cry, struggling to hold onto his hand.

"Iris!" Nate shouts. But the wind is too strong. Finger by finger, it drags us apart. I stumble to stay on my feet, getting further from Nate every second.

At last the wind dies down again. Yet it still holds me where I am – I can't reach Nate. I think we realise at the same moment that struggling won't help. We're trapped, held in place by the creature's will. I can see Nate's frustration. His hands are fists.

I glare at the tiny girl. I will *not* show her how much this bothers me.

"Much better," Sybil smirks. "Now, where were we? Ah, yes – your dreams!" She starts to pace in the moonlight. Her skin is so pale that it turns my stomach. It's like the belly of a dead fish.

"They're not dreams," she says. "They're memories. You see, you two are soul mates – you've had dozens of past lives together. Over and over. You just can't get enough of each other." She grimaces.

My startled gaze meets Nate's. Dreams about the Pyramids – about hiking in the snow – a hundred other places. 'Of course,' I think, in a daze. Not dreams. Memories.

Life after life together. It really *has* always been him.

"And as to who I am ..." Sybil sniggers and strikes a pose. "Well, I suppose you'd call me a demon. Or an evil spirit, if you were in a poetic mood."

She stops pretending to be amused then. "Soul mates," she spits out, as if the words taste bad. "Do you have any idea how rare that kind of love is? How special? So I decided to put a stop to it."

For a split second, her little-girl mask drops. My skin crawls – her real face looks like snakes twisting together. Then the little girl is back, glaring at us.

"I had *you* born in 1905, and *you* almost a hundred years later," Sybil says. She points to each of us in turn. "Problem solved, I thought. But your love is so strong that you still found each other, from a century away! You managed to find a time between times, where you could be together *again*, even if only for a few hours."

The creature sweeps a hand towards the house. For a moment her voice shakes with something like fear. Then she gains control again, and I think I must have been wrong.

"So that's when I stepped in to take over," she sneers. "This little game is being played by *my* rules now, kids."

Nate's arms are crossed over his chest. He looks at the creature in disgust. "Tell us what you want," he says flatly.

Sybil smiles. "Why, Nate, dear, I only want to tell you both about your futures. What's left of them. You might find it as amusing as I do."

I so don't want to hear anything that this creature thinks is funny. I'm beyond scared, but I try to hide it.

"Go on," I snap.

A snake slithers out of one of her eyes – she pulls it out and plays with it. "Oh, it's very jolly, I promise you," she says. "You see one or both of you is going to die tonight."

Sybil's sharp teeth gleam as she smiles at us. "Isn't that fun?"

～

The creature's words hang in the air. I stare at her in horror. She giggles and goes on. "And the *best* part is, after that you can't have any more lives together!"

"Please be so kind as to explain what the hell you're talking about," Nate says in a low voice.

Sybil shrugs. "It's simple. Time has stopped here. Very soon, I'm going to start it again. When I do, you'll both find yourselves outside the front gates, back in your own times. And those cars that almost hit you the last time you climbed over the gate? They'll kill you both this time. *Unless* one of you chooses to save the other by dying now, by my hand."

I swallow and glance at Nate. We have no reason to believe this creature ... yet, deep in the pit of my stomach, I know that she's telling the truth. From Nate's stunned expression, he knows it too.

Sybil sighs and twists a strand of her hair, pretending to be sad. "Of course, the one who lives will have to go on for ever without their true love. Because if you die in different times ... you can't come back together any more. Not ever. Isn't that a shame?"

I go cold as I imagine an eternity without Nate. Oh God, no – I only just found him again! But then I see something that makes me look at Sybil harder. I was right before ... I'm sure of it. Her black eyes hold a hint of fear.

Why would she be afraid? My mind races. I think back on all those times that I sensed something evil watching us. Like she was riveted by us, but hated us.

Nate's jaw looks carved in stone. "If I do what you ask, how can I trust you to keep your word?" he asks Sybil.

I gasp. He can't be considering this! "Nate, no!" I cry.

He doesn't look at me. I bite my lip in panic. There is no way – none – that the boy I know so well would ever let me be killed to save him. If he thinks there's a chance for me to live, he'll take it, no matter what.

Before Sybil can answer, I cut in. "Wait! Can I ask you something?" I blurt out the first thing that comes to mind. "How come we never saw you in any of our other lives? We didn't, did we? We just felt you, sometimes."

The creature's little-girl face glares at me. "Oh, I was there," she hisses. "But to take on a solid form around *you* two is –" She breaks off. For a split second, I see her fear again.

To take on a solid form around us is what? Difficult, maybe? Dangerous?

I can tell Nate knows I'm up to something. Then he looks at the well and frowns. He looks away again fast.

"All right, I want to talk terms," he says to Sybil. At the same time, he moves his head a bit as if to say, 'Iris, look over there.'

Sybil gives an evil giggle. "Oh, my terms are easy ... I'll set you loose, and then I'll kill you. It'll be slow and painful. I'm very good at that, you know."

I hardly hear her – because I've seen the same thing as Nate. There's a thin, pale cord trailing out of the well and across the grass. It leads right to the creature. It's the same colour as her skin.

And maybe it's a trick of the moonlight, but I'm sure I can see the cord shivering. As if it's ... alive.

I feel dizzy as I stare at it. All of a sudden I *know* what the cord leads to. Just like I've always *known* that I have to come to LA.

Some part of Sybil is still down there in that well.

I think fast. It has to be a part of her that she's trying to protect – something she needs in order to survive. If the love I share with Nate is really so special ... then could she fear it too much to even bring this part of her near it? Is *that* why she's scared?

My heart pounds. If I'm right, then this might be our only hope to destroy her. But *how*?

"I have to be sure that Iris will be safe," Nate is saying.

Sybil shrugs. "She'll be alive, at least. And then she can miss *you* for the rest of her life." A snake slithers out of her mouth and then back in again. "Ready to die, Nate?" She starts to raise her hand.

Oh God, I can't get this wrong! I gulp as I stare at the well. If there really is a part of her that could be destroyed by our love ... then what would happen to it if ...?

"You know, I always felt sorry for you," I say in a clear voice.

Sybil's head jerks towards me. "You *what?*" she snarls.

My lips are dry. I can feel the hatred pouring off her. I manage a shrug. "It's just that we'd sense you nearby sometimes. You always seemed so jealous. It made me feel bad for you."

The creature's mask slips again. The twisting snakes coil and hiss. "*Jealous?*" Her voice rises. "Of *what?*"

Nate jumps in. "Of the way we feel about each other, I guess. I always told Iris there was nothing we could do to help you. But she felt sorry for you anyway."

The creature's pointed teeth flash from the ball of snakes. "I don't need help!" she screams. "I am not jealous of you! I was *never* –"

The wind's screaming now, whipping at my hair – but for just a moment, I feel the creature's control slip. I don't stop to think. I break free and run for the well. I've got to get as close as I can to that part of her that can be hurt by our love.

Even when I know in my gut it's at the very bottom of the well.

'I love you, Nate,' I think, as hard as I can, as the well grows closer. 'I love you.'

"Stop!" Sybil cries. Her voice is full of fury ... and fear. The wind tries to pull me back, but already she's weaker.

"Iris!" I hear Nate's footsteps behind me. He knows exactly what I'm doing.

I don't stop. I reach the well and throw myself in.

As I jump, I feel Nate's strong arms around me. "You are *not* doing this alone," he gasps. I cling to him as we tumble downwards. We're both full of the same feeling, so powerful that it hurts. 'I love you – I love you –'

The water is gone now. On the rocky bottom of the well, there is a small grey lump. The cord leads right to it. The lump glows – I can see it beating.

It's the creature's heart.

As Nate and I hit it, the world seems to explode. He's passing through me – no, I'm passing through him. Which of us is a ghost? What time are we in? From somewhere far away I hear a terrible scream that's cut short ... and I know it's the creature. She's gone.

Blackness.

❧ 10 ❧

When I wake up, I'm lying on the grass.

At first I don't remember what's happened, and I blink up at the stars. What am I doing outside? And why can I smell oranges? Then it all comes rushing back. I sit up. My pulse beats hard as I look around but I can see only shadows.

I lick my lips. I'm afraid to say his name.

"Nate?" I whisper.

There's no answer. I feel as if I've been punched. "Nate!" This time I yell it as loud as I can. My voice echoes back to me.

Nothing. I slump down with my head in my hands, gasping as I struggle not to cry. We destroyed the evil spirit who hated us ... but did it even matter? We're still stuck in different times. We can never be together again – not in this life or any other.

Then I hear a low noise and I stiffen. Maybe the creature didn't die after all. I grope beside me to find some kind of weapon. My fingers close on a rock.

"Who's there?" I demand.

No answer. My heart thuds as I peer into the darkness. I expect any second to see that horrible snake-face coming at me. "Speak up, or get hit with a rock," I growl.

"Iris?" a groggy voice mumbles.

"*Nate!*" He's to the right of me, not far away. I drop the rock and crawl through the shadows until I find him. He's just sitting up, rubbing his head.

I grip his arms. He's real. He's here. "Are you OK?" I ask. "Please tell me you're OK!"

"Yeah, I'm fine, I just ..." Nate trails off, and his eyes widen in the faint moonlight. "Iris, is that really you? What am I saying, of course it's you – you just threatened to hit me!"

With a shaky laugh, he pulls me into his arms. *Nate.* I'm close to tears. I shut my eyes and press my face into his warm neck as we hold each other tight. I never want to let him go.

At last we pull apart a little. I clear my throat. "So ... where are we?" A terrible thought hits me. "We're not still in-between times, are we?"

Nate shakes his head. "No. Listen. You can hear the trees moving in the wind. We're in a real time now." He stops short, as if he's just realised what he's said. We stare at each other.

"A real time," I repeat. My heart starts to thud. "Nate!" I shriek. "We're in a real time – *the same one!*" I throw myself into his arms again and we tumble to the ground, laughing. We've done it! We've really done it.

Nate kisses my cheeks, my lips. "We'll never be apart again," he murmurs.

I'm almost too happy for words. "Maybe for tiny things," I say, and I kiss his nose. "Like, if one of us takes a shower or something."

He grins and flops onto his back. "Why should that keep us apart?" He wraps his arms around me. "The way I feel right now, I never want to let you out of my sight again."

I smile. "Even when I'm wet and soapy?"

He strokes my hair. "Then more than ever."

For a long time we just lie there, gazing at the stars and holding each other. When it starts getting colder, we rise to our feet. The cool night air whispers around us. The dark shape of the house looms up ahead, with the well in front of it. I shiver as I look at it.

"What even happened?" I ask. "We landed in the well, and then –"

"I don't know," Nate says. "I guess the blast blew us clear, or ... or who knows, really." He shakes his head, still staring at the well. "It's been a very odd day," he says at last.

I manage a weak laugh. "You can say that again. But were any parts of it good?"

Nate puts his hands on my shoulders and kisses me. He pretends to think about it. "Mmm. Parts of it have been just about OK."

I give his arm a mock punch. "Parts of it had better be much better than that."

He raises an eyebrow at me and grins. "The bee's knees, since you ask."

"Bee's knees?"

"Early 1920s slang. It means –"

"I think I can gather what it means," I say with a smile.

Then there's a pause, and we both look towards the gate. I can't tell from here whether it's still standing, like in Nate's time, or falling down, like in mine.

All of a sudden my mouth feels dry. The moon's gone behind a cloud now – the house is only a dark shape against the sky. I go and find my backpack where I dropped it, near the steps. Nate takes it from me and puts it over one shoulder.

"So ... I guess we should find out whose time we're in," I say.

Nate gazes towards the gate again. He nods, looking tense. He looks at me. "Do you, um ... do you mind if I hope it's mine?"

I shake my head. "Of course not! Nate, your family sound so nice. They'd be really worried about you."

But I wasn't sure what we'd do if it *was* Nate's time. How would he explain me to his parents? And in my time, I was a runaway and Nate hadn't even existed for years. That would be fun.

Nate takes my hand and we start down the dirt track. "If it's your time, that'll be all right too," he says, as if he can read my mind. "We'll handle whatever happens, Iris. The important thing is –" He squeezes my fingers between his. "This," he says. "Always."

My throat feels tight. "I know," I whisper. "We'll be all right. No matter what."

He brings my hand to his lips and kisses it. His fingers are warm and firm. Our footsteps echo as we walk towards the gate – mine, and those of the boy I've loved for more lifetimes than I can count.

Just before the gate comes into view, I smile.

"I wonder what we'll dream about now?" I say.

Our books are tested
for children and young people by
children and young people.

Thanks to everyone who consulted on
a manuscript for their time and effort in
helping us to make our books better
for our readers.

About the Author

Lee Weatherly was born in the USA in Little Rock, Arkansas. She was the youngest of three children and grew up in a house full of books. She always wanted to be a writer but had lots of other jobs first. Her favourite job was as a hostess at a ski resort in the alps – despite the fact she didn't know how to ski! She is very happy to be a writer now so she can work from home in her pyjamas if she wants to!

Lee has lived in the UK for almost 20 years. She lives in Hampshire with her husband and cat and goes for long walks and reads a lot. She's always been interested in Los Angeles and the idea of time travel ... so she couldn't resist writing about Iris and Nate, and thanks Barrington Stoke for making it happen.